Pick a Pup

For my puppy, Scout,
and all the pups who've ever
picked their person
—M. W. C.

For Tanei and the kid
—J. H.

MARGARET K. McELDERRY BOOKS • An imprint of
Simon & Schuster Children's Publishing Division •
1230 Avenue of the Americas, New York, New York
10020 • Text copyright © 2011 by Marsha Wilson
Chall • Illustrations copyright © 2011 by Jed Henry
All rights reserved, including the right of
reproduction in whole or in part in any form. •
MARGARET K. McELDERRY BOOKS is a trademark of
Simon & Schuster, Inc. • For information about
special discounts for bulk purchases, please contact
Simon & Schuster Special Sales at 1-866-506-1949 or
business@simonandschuster.com. • The Simon &
Schuster Speakers Bureau can bring authors to your
live event. For more information or to book an event,
contact the Simon & Schuster Speakers Bureau at
1-866-248-3049 or visit our website at
www.simonspeakers.com.
• Book design by Sonia Chaghatzbanian • The
text for this book is set in Malonia Voigo. • The
illustrations for this book are rendered in watercolor
and digitally. Manufactured in China • 1110 SCP
• Library of Congress Cataloging-in-Publication
Data • Chall, Marsha Wilson. • Pick a pup / Marsha
Chall ; illustrated by Jed Henry.–1st ed. • p. cm. •
Summary: After observing different types of dogs in
his neighborhood, Sam and Gram go to the local pet
shelter to choose a puppy. • ISBN 978-1-4169-7961-6
(hardcover) • [1. Stories in rhyme. 2. Dogs–Fiction.
3. Pets–Fiction. 4. Adoption–Fiction.]
I. Henry, Jed, ill. II. Title. • PZ8.3.C356Pi 2011 •
[E]–dc22 • 2009043243
2 4 6 8 10 9 7 5 3 1

FIRST
EDITION

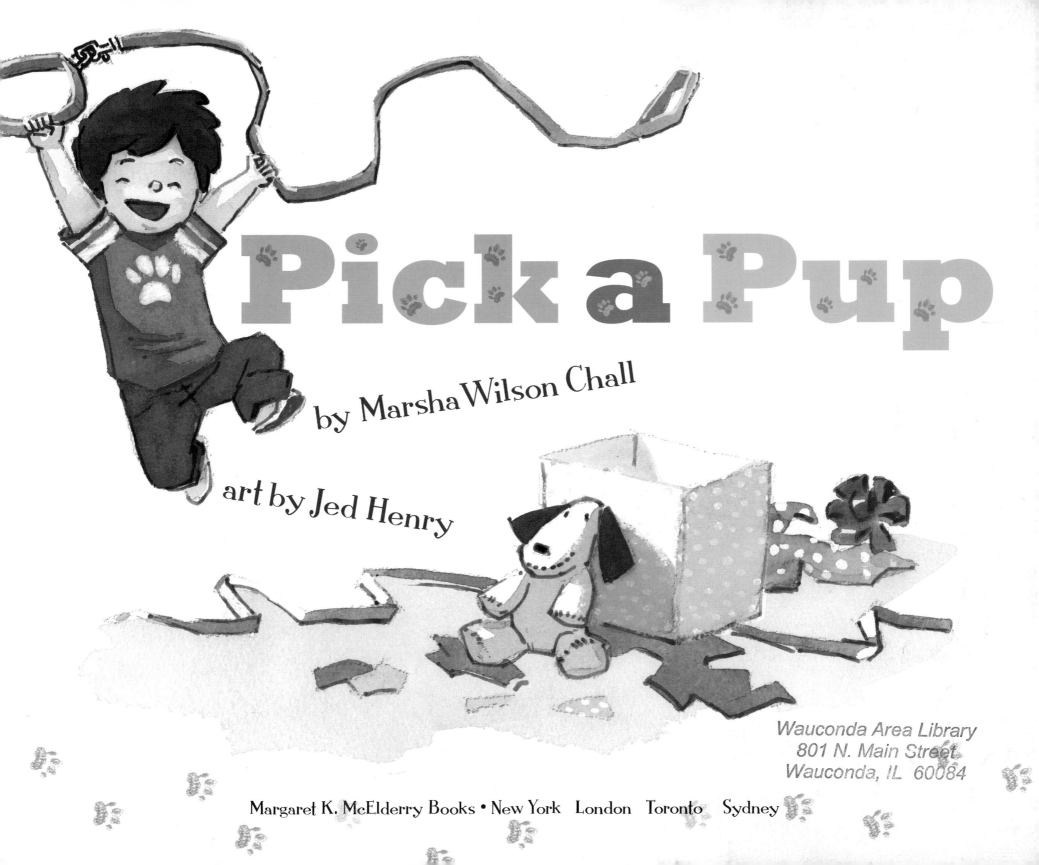

Pick a Pup

by Marsha Wilson Chall

art by Jed Henry

Margaret K. McElderry Books • New York   London   Toronto   Sydney

Sam can't wait to pick a pup.
But which one will he pick?
Is there a way to know the one—
a clue, a sign, a trick?

Eeny, meeny, miney, pup,

which teeny-weeny,

tiny pup?

"It's time to pick a pup," says Gram.
"A pup!" Sam says. "Let's go.

But will the shelter help me pick?"
Gram says, "I think you'll know."

Sam grabs a box and blanket.
It's not too far to walk.
Along the way they study dogs
from both sides of the block.

Mrs. Well's
sit-in-your-lap dog,

likes-to-take-a-nap dog,

hardly-makes-a-peep dog,

mostly-sound-asleep dog.

David's
runs-right-up pup,

always-wakes-you-up pup,

dances-for-a-bone pup,

hates-to-play-alone pup.

Mr. King's pedigreed-Who's-Who pup,

not-just-any-pup-will-do pup,

pick-of-the-litter pup,

not-a-sideline-sitter pup.

Ed and Joe's new pup,

a chew-an-old-shoe pup,

potluck-mix pup,

no-fancy-bag-of-tricks pup.

Auntie Ruth's woolly-like-a-sheep dog,

one-that-barks-down-deep dog,

loves-to-sniff-around dog,

nose-to-the-ground dog.

Kate's do-the-hokey-pokey pup,

never-lopey-mopey pup,

quick-lick-kissy pup,

pink-collar-little-missy pup.

Eeny, meeny, miney pup,

which teeny-weeny,

tiny pup?

"Sam," says Gram,
"we're almost there.
Soon you'll get to pick."
Sam gulps and wonders
how he will.
"Wish I knew the trick."

The shelter puppies bounce and play.
Each pup's a lot of fun.

"Gram," says Sam, "I want them all.
How can I pick just one?"

"Sam," says Gram,

"you picked a pup!"

Sam says, "We're meant to be."

Now Sam knows the trick's *who* picks—

"Gram, this pup picked me!"